ユーモアは世界を変える
英訳・今川乱魚のユーモア川柳

今川乱魚 著
速川美竹 訳

HUMOR CHANGES THE WORLD
The World of Imagawa Rangyo's Senryu

Shinyokan

FOREWORD

はじめに

Word, Word, Word

The morning glory
   Clings to the well bucket
I get water elsewhere.　　　KAGA-no-Chiyo

Trans. by R.H.Blyth

On a withered branch
   A crow is sitting
This autumn eve.　　　MATUO Basho

Trans. by W.G.Aston

Poverty also,
   In excess,—
And they laugh together.　　　YOSHIKAWA Kijiro

Trans. by R.H.Blyth

The snow-clad roofs
   Are getting hungry
For rumor and gossip.　　　MINAKAWA Ayako

Trans. by Mitake

　The former two quoted above are called haiku, and the latter two senryu. They are historically relat-

言葉・ことば・コトバ

朝顔につるべとられて貰い水

　　　　　　　　　　　　加賀　千代

枯枝にからすとまりけり秋のくれ

　　　　　　　　　　　　松尾　芭蕉

貧しさも余りの果ては笑い合い

　　　　　　　　　　　　吉川雉子郎

雪の屋根うわさ話に飢えている

　　　　　　　　　　　　皆川　綾子

　冒頭に引用した句の前の2句は俳句で、後の2句は川柳です。歴史的には両者は関連があり、1

HUMOR CHANGES THE WORLD

ed and composed in three units of 5, 7, 5 syllables each. In principle haiku are composed mainly about nature (fortunately Japan is blessed with four seasons), and senryu about human beings. The three elements required for the classical senryu used to be considered 'lightness, penetrating insight, and wit or humor'. Since our thinking, feeling and life-style today have become quite complicated, however, new types of senryu naturally have emerged in order to add a modern spirit. Those who live in this busy and heartless world should carefully observe and keenly criticicize the world by using the satire and humor characteristic of senryu.

Some compose senryu in one line and some in three. And in this book, the translator chose the latter form; and besides made more of the true meaning of senryu than of its rhythm. I hope that you will remember that senryu is, though alike, but different from what is called 'kyoku' or 'joking verse' which often contains obscene jokes or mere wordplay in it.

The translator as well as the author has been trying to compose "modern senryu". It is a matter of regret, however, that the author passed away while

句が5,7,5音節の3行で成り立っています。俳句は原則として、(幸いにして四季に恵まれている日本ですので)主として自然を詠み、川柳は人間を詠みます。昔は「軽味」「穿ち」「笑い」が川柳の3要素と言われていましたが、人間の考え方、感じ方、生活様式が複雑多様になった今日では、当然のこととして近代性を盛り込んだ新しい形の川柳が現われてきました。忙しく、思いやりのない現在の世の中に生きる人々は、この川柳独特の風刺とユーモアを応用して世の中を注意深く観察し、且つ鋭く批判すべきでしょう。

　川柳を1行で表す人もいれば、3行で表わす人もいます。本書では後者を選び、不十分ながら句の意味内容を重視しました。最後に、川柳は、しばしば下がかった笑いや駄洒落を含むいわゆる「狂句」とは似て非なるものだということを忘れないでいただきたいのです。

　最後に、著者も翻訳者も以上のことを考慮しながら、日頃から現代にふさわしい川柳を発表して

awaiting the publication of this book, soon after retirement from the ex-president of the Japan Senryu Association.

Last of all, I'd like to offer an expression of thanks to Ms.Elizabeth Shinagawa for her advice, and especially to Mr.William I. Elliott, Professor Emeritus of Kanto Gakuin University, for his supervision.

HAYAKAWA MITAKE
(Senryu Poet)

きましたが、哀しいことに著者である(社)全日本川柳協会前会長は本書の出版を待たずして逝去しました。

　終わりにエリザベス・シナガワさんと、校閲して頂いた関東学院大学名誉教授のウイリアム・エリオット先生に感謝の意を表したいと思います。

2011年3月

速川　美竹
(川柳家)

HUMOR CHANGES THE WORLD
― The World of Imagawa Rangyo's Senryu ―

By Imagawa Rangyo
Trans. By Hayakawa Mitake

ユーモアは世界を変える
―英訳・今川乱魚のユーモア川柳―

Talk of love
　　And talk of money
　　Don't mesh.

愛の話と銭の話は嚙み合わぬ

The position
    Of the fig leaf
        Is hard to change.

いちじくの葉っぱの位置は動かせぬ

Once in a while
We feel drowsy
While praying.

祈ってるうちに眠気に襲われる

Come to think of it,
    Only a few
        Wish me to live long.

生きていてくれというのはひと握り

Some people begin
　　To chat standing
　　　　At the reception desk.

　　　　受付の前で始まる立ち話

On a festival day
  I bought the most fearsome mask
   At a booth.

縁日で一番恐い面を買う

The child gives a chilly glance
　　At his father
　　　　Playing the fool for him.

おどけてる父へ子の目がさめている

My boyfriend was nice enough
　To invite me
　　To sleep in the same grave.

同じ墓に入ろうというプロポーズ

The verbal promise

　　With a woman is

　　　　To keep you on a chain.

　　　　女との口約束は鉄鎖

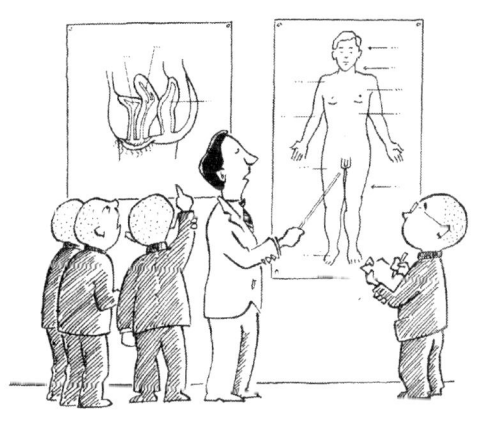

Carefully observed
　On an anatomical chart
　　The male body is boring.

男とはつまらぬものよ人体図

Even Superman
Catches cold
In old age.

スーパーマン老いてはすぐに風邪をひく

Patients are bursting
　　To waste money
　　　　On the road to recovery.

回復期うずうず金が使いたし

On Tuesday workers hustle
For money, and on Friday
They will need it.

火曜には燃え金曜に金がいる

When I sing a parody
 I refresh myself
  Before I know it.

替え歌を唄うと元気湧いてくる

I go out for a walk
　　Just like a king
　　　　With my pet dog in tow.

　　　　王様の気分で犬を従える

Arranged in a line
    Even cosmetics pose
        On a dressing table.

鏡台に並べばビンもポーズする

Love begins by kissing
  And ends
   By running down the other.

キッスから始まり罵倒して終り

A dog appears starved
    With the mate to shoes
    In his mouth.

口寂しい犬だな靴をくわえてる

I focused my eyes on a gravure
Of a girl in a bathing suit
As if by accident.

グラビアの水着にピタリ目が止まる

Some Japanese
    Can't blind others
        Without using English.

煙に巻くときに英語をちらつかす

There's an alluring peepholes
In a board of the fence
At a construction site.

工事中の塀にやさしいのぞき穴

People are kept waiting
    Too often by doctors
        And lovers as well.

恋人にも医者にもやたら待たされる

HUMOR CHANGES THE WORLD

A day without love
> Is just like Christmas
>> Without any candles.

恋なきは灯のなき如しクリスマス

By rascals named Justice
> Numerons people are killed
> Day after day.

正義という曲者今日も人が死ぬ

I'm to blame
　　For at least half
　　　　Of my wife's wrinkles.

　　妻の皺半分ほどの責めを負う

Now I remember well
   My left arm
      Serving as my wife's pillow.

妻の枕にしたこともある左腕

The sound of the shower
　　My wife is taking
　　　　Sounds melodious to me.

妻のいるシャワーの音がやわらかい

The nearer to Heaven
　　The more quickly
　　　　The hair falls out.

天国に近い髪から抜けていく

Next to the ceiling
    A woman's charming legs
        Catch my eyes.

　　　天井の次に見るのは脚線美

The color of an IV drip
　　Reminds me of amber whisky
　　With water or with lemon.

点滴の色に水割りレモン割り

I let my close friends
　　Know the contents
　　　　Of my purse beforehand.

友達に財布の底も見せておく

Doing a quiz
    Halfway, at last
        I've peeked its answer.

途中まで書いて答えを見るクイズ

I know how to beat time
With my hands
Matching any song.

どの歌にも合う手拍子をもっている

Through an endoscope
    I see my stomach
        Throb indecently.

内視鏡胃はワイセツに脈を打つ

Owing to a long life
Some can forecast
The weather favorably.

長生きをしてお天気をよく当てる

Mother manages
   About household chores
      With her ten hands.

母は手を十本もって家事こなす

Holding our noses,
We actually feel
We are still alive.

鼻つまむと生きているのがすぐ判る

On happy days
 I always ride
  The first car.

ハイの日の電車一番前に乗る

We see the advent of God
　　During the performance
　　　Of the pipe organ.

　　　パイプオルガンで神様降りてくる

Before getting out
   Of the comfortable bed
      I have lost my motivation.

ふかふかのベッドに置いて来たガッツ

Many adventures are called off
Soon after an outfit
　　Has already been prepared.

冒険は道具そろえたとこでやめ

A bossa nova
　　　And a strained back.
　　　　　Are perfect strangers.

ボサノバとざっくり腰は縁がない

Two bookworms
　　Meet each other
　　　　At a bookstore.

本の虫二匹本屋の待ち合わせ

A hat turned upside down
   Is flooded
      With goodwill.

帽子裏返せば善意降り注ぎ

Even under anesthesia
No one will divulge his woman's name
No matter what happens.

　　　麻酔かけられてもいえぬ女の名

It's next to impossible
    To let those living
        On water return money.

水を飲む人から金は取りにくい

Some men are longing
　　To go to Paris
　　　　Where they are called Monsieur.

　　　ムッシューと呼ばれるパリに憧れる

As often as I see
    Munck's *The Scream*
        I suppress a yawn.

ムンク叫ぶ口へあくびを噛み殺す

Blood and urine
　　Taken for a test
　　　　No one takes tears.

　　採血採尿涙は誰も採りに来ぬ

I wore pajamas
  Of the color of the sea
    For the medical examination.

検査日のパジャマに海の色選ぶ

Whatever parts of the stomach
I may be operated on
I have nothing to be ashamed of.

腹のどこ切ろうと恥じるものはなし

Without good-by
 I had a sad parting
  From my spleen.

挨拶もなく脾臓とは別れたり

Apparently some come
　To the hospital with a mission
　　To observe patients' conditions.

　　偵察の任務を帯びて来た見舞い

Relying on an IV drip
   Internal organs
      Ceased to work.

点滴に頼り臓器が怠け出す

The dimples of a nurse
　　　Laughing cheerfully
　　　　　Give me peace of mind.

　　　よく笑うナースの笑窪から癒える

I just tried to search
  An anatomical chart
    For my removed internal organs.

喪った臓器をさがす人体図

A TV comercial for beer
Will only attract attention
Because our stomachs are healthy.

　　　　胃があってこそをビールのコマーシャル

I recovered from cancer
　　Before going
　　　　To heaven or hell.

天国も地獄も見ずに癌癒える

I am determined to live
Ten years longer to recover
The cost of the operation.

十年は生きて手術の元を取る

If I shoud have a flat stomach
　Hospitalization
　　Will have been very successful.

腹が引っ込めば入院もうけもの

Nothing is written
　　But the disposal of old books
　　In the will.

　　　古本の処分のほかに遺書はなし

Every night I see
　　Bacchus I promised
　　　　Never to do again.

指切りをしたバッカスと夜毎会う

No one has seen
　　　Christ laugh
　　　　　In any sacred pictures.

キリストの笑う絵をまだ見ていない

Every time the whistle sounds
　My life takes
　　A different direction.

笛が鳴る度に人生向きを変え

Before I line it
　　With a red pencil
　　　　The book is not mine.

　　赤線を引いてわたしの本となる

Before I leave a museum
    I return to my favorite picture
      Once again.

美術展出口で好きな絵に戻り

Anyone has engaged
　In printing counterfeit bills
　　More than once in dreams.

贋札を一度は夢で刷っている

Somehow or other
  My back itches —
    Wings might grow there.

背のかゆみ翼が生えてくるのかも

It occurs to me
    That I wish to eat
        The women Renoir drew.

ルノワールの女を食べてみたくなる

Many of the fables
    Saints once told
        Are too good to be true.

聖者らのたとえ話がうますぎる

Whenever I see a new movie
I want to read
One original after another.

映画化のたびあれを読みこれを読み

Looking up at the blue sky
 I feel like taking
  A day off from work.

青い空―口会社休もうか

At first I never used
　　This camera without taking
　　　　The pictures of my wife.

　　妻ばかり最初はとっていたカメラ

My nose brings home
    The sunlight
        Of Iberia with me.

イベリアの陽ざしを鼻に持ち帰り

Man and woman
   Hold something soft
      Named love in their palms.

愛というやわらかきもの掌に包む

To my regret,
On kissing a brnad-new bill
I have to say good-bye.

ピン札に口づけをしてさようなら

I will always sit down
　　On the edge of a chair
　　　　So I can run away any time.

腰浅く掛けていつでも逃げ出そう

Following the red arrow,
 I'm sure
  To see you smiling.

 矢印の先に笑顔の君がいる

There stands a gravestone
　　With the epitaph inscribed
　　　"Here sleeps love."

恋ここに眠ると書いて石を置く

My wife and I
> Are not always buried
>> In the same tomb.

妻が同じ墓に入るとは限らない

Why don't we part
　　From each other,
　　　　Pulling down the full moon?

　　　　満月を引きずりおろし別れよう

Old soldiers never die,
 Never die;
  They only draw their pension.

老兵は死なず年金受けている

If you should pay compliment
One million times,
I'll let you take a good position.

百万遍お世辞言ったら椅子をやる

If I could tranform myself
   Into a bird, I'm willing
      To stop working for wages.

鳥になれたらサラリーマンは即やめる

I never overlook Alain Delon
Playing a villan
In any films.

悪役のアランドロンが許せない

Nothing is more effective
　　For my weary eyes
　　　　Than seeing blue films.

疲れ日に何とよく利くポルノかな

When the music has stopped
My seat
Was already occupied.

音楽が止まりわたしの椅子がない

I have chosen beforehand
    Whom to ask
        What the flower is called.

化の名を聞くべき人を決めておく

A patient feels pain
　　Knowing his favorite nurse
　　Loves someone else.

　　　看護婦の恋もうすうす知って病む

With all the pores unblocked
   I'm looking forward
      To seeing friends from afar.

毛穴全開遠方の友を待つ

The sounds of angel's wings
Have not been heard
For a long time.

エンゼルの羽音しばらく聞いてない

A girlfriend is apt
    To bring up his salary
        Even after kisses.

口づけのあと年収に触れてくる

After running my eyes
　　Over works of art
　　　　Suddenly I feel hungry.

　　芸術をひとわたり見て腹が減り

I'd be ready
    To help you rebuild
        The rainbow some time.

手を貸そう虹の架け替え工事なら

In Japan, the tax deadline
　Falls
　　In the most beautiful season.

美しい日本の四季に納税期

How many useless adjectives
　Are used
　　　In scolding children!

子を叱る言葉にむだな形容詞

Out of pride
　I consult a dictionary
　　Taking care not to be caught.

　　自尊心こっそり辞書をひいてみる

Man does wrong
> Using the wisdom
>> Granted by God.

神様にもらった知恵で悪事する

Somehow, eating soup
 Noisily
  Makes the soup taste better.

音たてて飲むとスープの味がする

After a promotion
> The first business card I gave
> Was to my wife.

昇格の名刺一枚妻に出し

I would invent lies
　　Without sleeping a wink
　　　　So I can get a date.

逢うための嘘なら寝ずに考える

The number of handshakes
With many people
Is all in all to me.

握手した数がわたしの宝もの

With the cherry-blossoms
In full bloom
Japanese men easily play the fool.

　　　花の下男は阿呆になり切れる

I gaze at the woman
   From behind,too,
      I expect to make my wife.

妻にする女はうしろからも見る

The opinion was so right
That few
　　　Clapped their hands.

正論にだんだん減ってゆく拍手

This dictionary
 Almost falling apart
  Is my "second brain."

よれよれの辞書を第二の脳とする

We drink at an underground bar
And later leave
To breathe oxygen later.

地下街で飲んで酸素を吸いに出る

At any age
>   Boys tame a dinosaur
>   In their hearts.

少年の胸恐竜を飼いならす

In a pause while reading
A novel I answered
My wife curtly.

小説の切れ目で妻に返事する

Remembering stars
One by one
I feel drowsy.

惑星を順に覚えて眠くなり

I fixed the day
For hospitalization
After a haircut.

散髪をすませ入院日を決める

However many lullabies
    I may hear,
        I can't get to sleep.

子守唄いくつ聞いても寝付かれず

While patients are asleep
The surgeons
Are drenched in sweat.

眠らせておく間に医師の大仕事

I'm willing to make
> The rounds of hospitals
> If I can linger on.

生きるためなら病院のはしごする

Cancer is not such a mild disease
Not any hymn
Can cure it.

讃美歌の歌詞に静まる癌でない

Counting backward from the expense
Of the operation
I draw money out of the bank.

手術から逆算をして金おろす

Before presenting my wife
With a dress
I size her up.

プレゼント妻のサイズを目で測る

Throughout
 The Middle East
  Gods fight one another.

多神教神もワンノブゼムである

HUMOR CHANGES THE WORLD

Copying what others say
　　We manage
　　　　To get along in the world.

　　　耳学問の受け売りをして世を渡り

Human beings
　Mark the countdown
　　Till they are turned to dust.

土になる日までをカウントダウンする

After shaking hands
I return them
To my warm pockets.

握手した手がポケットにあるぬくみ

I can easily tell my wife
From my daughter
By the way the door is unlocked.

鍵の音妻と娘を聞き分ける

When a rainbow
    Appears in the sky
        I always skip home.

虹が出た日はスキップをして帰り

All the family members
Gather together and warmly
Discuss what to name a stray cat.

野良猫の名を家中で考える

No matter how often
　　You gaze out to sea
　　　　You can hardly save money.

　　　海ばかり見てても金は溜まらない

When sunflowers are in bloom
The whole garden
Refresh itself.

ひまわりが咲き庭中が元気づき

Once a word is uttered
It is impossible
To take it back.

口から出た言葉が口へ戻れない

The sight of a round peach
Allows me to cherish
A delusion.

妄想を桃の丸みが掻き立てる

Not until the special guests had left
Could the celebration
Be complete.

来賓が帰って弾む祝賀会

In appearance,
   Geniuses' heads are the same
   As anyone else's.

天才の脳もみかけは変わらない

あとがき

　本書に掲載された原句の作者・今川乱魚氏は日本の柳界に惜しまれながら2010年4月に天国に行ってしまいました——親交があったので、以下「乱魚さん」と呼ばせて頂きます。乱魚さんは巻末の略歴でも分かる通り、日本川柳界の指導者として人生に終止符を打たれましたが、そのめざましい足跡は遺された多くの著書が如実に物語ってくれています。

　彼は単に一人で川柳を楽しむだけではなく、その楽しみを不案内の人に広めるため、定年前から心身を削って活動を続け、苦労をいとわず一家言ある川柳家の組織を支えて来たことは衆目の一致するところです。自らが創設した大きな結社を、育て上げた後継者に淡々として譲り渡し、不治の病である癌との闘いに挑みながら、研究会、句会、勉強会などを続け、「生きるためなら病院のはしごする」経過までをも句にまとめて、同病の士に笑いと勇気を与えまし

た。『癌と闘う―ユーモア川柳乱魚句集』は実に「負けてたまるか」「性懲りもなく」という2章から成り立っており、度重なる手術の経験から、病人の心境を詠むには「ありのままの人間を詠む」ことだと断じています。

「川柳が客観句であろうが、主観句であろうが、喜怒哀楽のすべてを対象として読まれる文芸」であると理解していた乱魚さんは、「ありのままの人間」を掬いあげ、「周囲を笑いの渦に巻き込み、心の平和をもたらし、自分自身をも元気づける」といった句を詠み続けました。マーク・トウェインは、ユーモアがなければ天国へは行きたくないと言ったそうですが、「もし川柳から笑いがきえるようなことがあれば、それは人間性の後退」という乱魚さんの言葉と相通ずるものがあると思います。しかしマスメディアの川柳への無理解を見て、乱魚さんは「弱者や他人の欠点を笑うのがユーモアであると勘違いしている人もいるが、それはまったくの誤りである」と釘を刺すことを忘れていませんでした。

子どもの時に父君が戦死したおかげで貧乏生活をしたが、吉川雉子郎の句ではないが「貧しさもあまりの果は笑い合い」という気持ちで前向きに人生を歩み、父親を奪った戦争というものを憎み、「靖国神社

には参拝しない」(『銭の音』)という反骨も貫きました。そういう点は、「妻ばかり最初はとっていたカメラ」時代から、「妻の皺半分ほどの責めを負う」と言いたくなるほど晩年は苦労をかけた奥さんへの愛情句と共に、乱魚さん自らが選んだユーモア句で直接に接して理解して頂きたいものです。

　最後に、ずっと以前、財団法人経済広報センターの行革キャンペーンとして川柳を取り上げたとき以来の関係で元経済団体連合会事務総長で全日本川柳協会顧問の三好正也氏に生前「序文」をお願いしていたことをこの度初めて知ったが、それから4年も経過し、種々事情も変わったので、出版社と話し合った末、失礼ながら割愛させて頂いたことを報告し、著者に代わり感謝を申し上げる次第です。生前に本書が完成しなかったのは、ひとえに多忙と老化のせいで引き延ばした訳者の責任であり、今やお会いできなくなった乱魚さんに心からお詫びする次第です——さぞやご自分でユーモアと含蓄のある「あとがき」を満足げにお書きになりたかったことでしょうに、合掌！

2011年1月1日

速川美竹

【訳者略歴】

速川美竹 (はやかわ・みたけ)

立正大学名誉教授
日本英学史学会顧問（元会長）
日本ペンクラブ会員
川柳レモンの会・九品仏川柳会代表

著著
『速川美竹の英訳川柳　開けごま』（柳都川柳社）
『国際化した日本の短詩』3名共著（中外日報社）
『現代川柳ハンドブック』8名共編執筆（雄山閣）
『小泉八雲の世界』（笠間書院）
『英学の祖オレゴンのマクドナルド』2名共訳（雄松堂）
『英語の常識・非常識』（講談社）
『英語パズル』（講談社）
『Q＆A英語なんでも情報辞典』3名共編執筆（研究社）
『英語教材のいずみ（英語教育シリーズ5）』3名共著
『名文章名表現辞典』2名共編（小学館）

その他、辞典。論文多数。

【著者略歴】

今川乱魚（いまがわ・らんぎょ）

　1935年東京生まれ。本名充。早稲田大学法学部卒。

　大阪で川柳を始める。999番傘川柳会会長。東葛川柳会最高顧問。東京みなと番傘川柳会元会長、番傘川柳本社幹事。(社) 全日本川柳協会会長。日本川柳ペンクラブ常任理事。川柳人協会顧問。北國新聞、リハビリテーション川柳欄、川柳マガジン「笑いのある川柳」選者。千葉、東京で川柳講座講師。

　第3回日本現代詩歌文学館館長賞、第9回川柳・大雄賞、第40回川柳文化賞受賞。

　著書に『乱魚川柳句文集』、『ユーモア川柳乱魚句集』『癌と闘う―ユーモア川柳乱魚句集』、『銭の音―ユーモア川柳乱魚句集』『妻よ―ユーモア川柳乱魚句文集』、『癌を睨んで―ユーモア川柳乱魚ブログ』、『ユーモア川柳乱魚ブログⅡ』、『川柳作家全集　今川乱魚』。編著に『川柳贈る言葉』、『川柳ほほ笑み返し』、『科学大好き―ユーモア川柳乱魚選集』科学編・技術編・生活編、『三分間で詠んだ―ユーモア川柳乱魚選集』、『李琢玉川柳句集　酔牛』『岸本水府の川柳と詩想』。

　住　所：千葉県柏市逆井1167-4（〒277-0042）

HUMOR CHANGES THE WORLD

Imagawa Rangyo
HUMOR CHANGES THE WORLD
― The World of Imagawa Rangyo's Senryu ―

Trans. By Hayakawa Mitake

publishing office
Shinyokan-Publication
9-16,Tamatsukuri 1-chome,Higashinari-ku,
Osaka 537-0023 Japan

ユーモアは世界を変える
― 英訳・今川乱魚のユーモア川柳 ―
○
2011年3月26日　初版

著者
今 川 乱 魚

訳者
速 川 美 竹

発行人
松 岡 恭 子

発行所
新 葉 館 出 版
大阪市東成区玉津1丁目9-16 4F 〒537-0023
TEL06-4259-3777　FAX06-4259-3888
http://shinyokan.ne.jp

印刷所
BAKU WORKS
○
定価はカバーに表示してあります。
©Imagawa Sachiko Printed in Japan 2011
本書からの転載には出所を記してください。業務用の無断複製を禁じます。
ISBN978-4-86044-430-3